Joseph Willard

Naturalization in the American Colonies

SALZWASSER
VERLAG

Joseph Willard

Naturalization in the American Colonies

Reprint of the original, first published in 1859.

1st Edition 2022 | ISBN: 978-3-37513-310-8

Verlag (Publisher): Salzwasser Verlag GmbH, Zeilweg 44, 60439 Frankfurt, Deutschland
Vertretungsberechtigt (Authorized to represent): E. Roepke, Zeilweg 44, 60439 Frankfurt, Deutschland
Druck (Print): Books on Demand GmbH, In de Tarpen 42, 22848 Norderstedt, Deutschland

NATURALIZATION

IN THE

AMERICAN COLONIES,

WITH MORE PARTICULAR REFERENCE TO MASSACHUSETTS.

A Paper read before the Massachusetts Historical Society, at the July Meeting, 1859.

BY JOSEPH WILLARD.

— — —

BOSTON:
PRINTED BY JOHN WILSON AND SON,
22, School Street.

1859.

TRACTATE.

THE hostility of ancient nations to aliens, connected more or less closely with the sentiment of race and of patriotism, and made more intense by diversity of language, continued with few exceptions through the various periods of their history, and passed into modern Europe in its several centuries, uninfluenced to any extent by the progress of civilization and refinement, and the precepts of Christianity.

At the present day, though this hostility may be considered as at an end, a distinctive feeling between citizens of the same country and aliens continues, and will never be eradicated while men are separated into distinct communities.

In the following tractate, it is not proposed to discuss the doctrines embraced in the change or transfer of allegiance, or to consider any real or supposed modifications of what have been regarded as the legitimate results of those doctrines, but, only as a matter pertaining to our own history, to give a summary of the English statutes touching naturalization, followed by references to some of the Colonial charters and laws, especially to the exercise of jurisdiction in the Province of Massachusetts Bay, and in the Commonwealth both before and after the adoption of the Constitution of the United States.

In no country of Europe has the exclusion of foreigners been more strictly enforced than in England; so that, until a recent period, no one could become a British subject except by a special Act of Parliament.* In addition to the reasons given above, the pride of the Anglo-Saxon race, which hardly permits an Englishman to look on his Continental neighbor as an equal, would lead him to regard with dread any encroachment upon a population that had become homogeneous in the progress of centuries,—a dread that would not be diminished by the narrow channel that divides him from other races.

But, while she guarded the sea-girt isle with this extreme jealousy, she was, as will be seen in the context, more liberal towards her Colonies after they began to acquire assured strength; that is to say, more liberal as regarded foreign Protestants, while wholly excluding the Roman Catholic from every privilege of a subject.

The first relaxation of the ancient restriction took place in 1708, under statute 7 Anne, chap. 5, entitled " AN ACT FOR NATURALIZING FOREIGN PROTESTANTS." The preamble states the plain proposition, that " the increase of a people is a means of advancing the wealth and strength of a nation;" and adds, that "many strangers of the Protestant or Reformed religion, out of a due consideration of the happy constitution of the government of this realm, would be induced to transport themselves and their estates into this kingdom, if they might be made partakers of the advantages and privileges which the natural-born subjects thereof do enjoy." It is then enacted, that all persons taking the oaths, and making

---

* By the statute of 7 and 8 Victoria, chap. 66, a resident alien subject of a friendly State, or one who shall hereafter come to reside in any part of the United Kingdom with intent to settle therein, desirous of being naturalized, is required to set forth, in a memorial to one of the principal Secretaries of State, the facts concerning his age, profession, or occupation, length of residence, &c. If the secretary, after examination, is satisfied of the truth of the memorial, he may issue a certificate, granting to the alien, on his taking the prescribed oaths, *all the rights of a natural-born subject,* except that of being a member of Parliament or of the Privy Council, and any other exceptions especially named in the certificate; which certificate must be enrolled in the Court of Chancery.

This statute did not extend to the Colonies. See statute 10 and 11 Victoria, chap. 83, enacted in 1847, cited *post.*

and subscribing the declaration appointed by statute 6 Anne, chap. 23, and having received the sacrament of the Lord's Supper in some Protestant congregation within three months, shall be deemed natural-born subjects.

This law did not extend to the Colonies, and did not find favor at home. Parliament soon relapsed into the old stringent doctrine of the common law, and in 1711, after an experiment of three years, repealed the statute of 7 Anne, because, according to the preamble, " divers mischiefs and inconveniences have been found by experience to follow from the same, to the discouragement of the natural-born subjects of this kingdom, and to the detriment of the trade and wealth thereof." The " discouragement and detriment " may have been more in seeming than in fact; but so it was, that this exclusion of foreigners remained as of old in the mother country until the present reign.

But there were other statutes designed for the benefit of the Colonies, where it was supposed the " discouragement and detriment " complained of at home would not exist. In several of the Colonies, foreign Protestants had become numerous, and their numbers were rapidly increasing; and thus it had become a very desirable object to attach them to their new homes, by giving them an interest in the soil, and admitting them to full civil and political privileges, so that agriculture and trade and general wealth might be developed. To this end, in 1740, the statute 13 George II., chap. 7, was passed, with a preamble similar to that of 7 Anne: viz., that " the increase of a people is a means of advancing the wealth and strength of any nation or country; and that many foreigners and strangers, from the lenity of our government, the purity of our religion, the benefit of our laws, the advantages of our trade, and the security of our property, might be induced to come and settle in some of his majesty's Colonies in America, if they were made partakers of the advantages and privileges which the natural-born subjects of this realm do enjoy."

This statute admitted all Protestant foreigners to the privileges of natural-born subjects, on a residence of seven years in any one of the Colonies, without an absence exceeding two months at any one time, taking the oaths of allegiance, abjuration, &c., and receiving the sacrament, &c. The oaths and declarations — with exceptions in favor of Quakers and Jews — were required to be taken before a judge in open court, between nine and twelve o'clock in the forenoon; and to be entered in the same court, and also in the secretary's office of the Colony. The judge was required to make a due and proper entry of the oaths, &c., " in a book to be kept for that purpose in said court; " and the secretary was required to make the like entry in a like book to be kept for the same purpose in his office, upon notification by the judge.

A certificate, under the Colonial seal, was full proof of naturalization.

The secretary was directed to transmit to the office of the Commissioners for Trade and Plantations, annually, the names of all who had taken the benefit of the act.

Naturalized persons could not be of the Privy Council or of Parliament; or hold any office or place of trust, civil or military, in Great Britain or Ireland; or hold real estate within the same by grant from the crown.*

In 1747, by statute 20 George II., chap. 44, the benefits of the statute of 1740 were extended to the " Moravian Brethren, and other foreign Protestants, not Quakers, who conscientiously scruple the taking of an oath; many of whom are settled in the Colonies." They are described as a "sober, quiet, and industrious people; " and it is added, that "many others of the like persuasion are desirous to transport themselves thither."

---

* This clause in the statute was repealed by statute 13 George III., chap. 33, so far as concerned holding office or taking crown grants of land, except within the kingdom of Great Britain and Ireland. The repeal extends to the subsequent statutes recited below.

The statute 29 George II., chap. 5, enacted in 1756, recites that many foreign Protestants have been induced by the statute of 1740 to settle in some of the Colonies, "particularly in the Provinces of Maryland and Pennsylvania; the natural-born subjects of which last-mentioned Province do in great part consist of the people called Quakers, whose backwardness in their own defence exposes themselves and that part of America to imminent danger." On this account, provision is made for raising a regiment of four battalions, of one thousand men each, into which naturalized foreigners may be enlisted; and a certain number of foreigners who have served abroad as officers or engineers may be appointed to serve in the regiment, on taking the oaths, &c., as prescribed in the former statutes. The colonel of the regiment must be "a natural-born subject, and not any person naturalized or made a denizen."

In 1761, statute 2 George III., chap. 25, these officers were duly remembered. They had raised "a great number of men, and trained them to discipline as soldiers." Several of the officers had "purchased estates in the Colonies, and had given the strongest assurances of their attachment and fidelity to the British Government." On these grounds, and to induce others, then or thereafter settled in America, "to engage in his majesty's service," it provided "that all such foreign Protestants, as well officers as soldiers, who have served or shall hereafter serve in the Royal-American regiment,* or as engineers in America, for the space of two years, and shall take and subscribe the oaths, and make, repeat, and subscribe the declaration, &c., . . . shall be deemed . . . his majesty's natural-born subjects of this kingdom."

---

* General Gates, a native of England, was a major in the Royal Americans. At an earlier period in the French War, he was captain of a New-York Independent Company which served in the campaign of Braddock. He was severely wounded in the battle in which Braddock was defeated. In 1772, he emigrated to Virginia, and purchased an estate in Berkeley County.

The foregoing enumeration embraces all the English statute provisions in relation to naturalization in the Colonies
preceding the Revolution. They are sufficiently liberal in
term of residence required; and probably many foreign Protestants, in several of the Colonies, sought for the benefits
opened by these statutes. But in Massachusetts, where the
population was well-nigh homogeneous and Puritan, it was
otherwise. In the Court of Common Pleas for the County
of Suffolk, not one instance of naturalization is to be found
from 1740 to 1752. Whether there were any between 1752
and the Revolution cannot be ascertained, as the records
for the whole of that period are and have been missing
from the office ever since the evacuation of Boston, in
March, 1776.*

The records of the Superior Court of the Province for
all the Counties are kept in the office of the Clerk of the
Supreme Court, in Boston; and it is remarkable, as the result
of a careful search which I directed to be made from 1740 up
to the Revolution, that only four persons were naturalized in
that court.† No book, such as the judge was required to
keep, is to be found; and there is none in the office of the
Secretary of State. The only persons naturalized under these
laws were Nicholas Budd, Aaron Lopez, Emanuel Peraro, and
Theodore Dehon.

The following is an abstract of the record in each case: —

---

* At one time, it was thought that they were in Halifax, N.S.; and an early effort
was made to find them, but in vain. The late William C. Aylwin, Esq., when clerk,
met with no better success. Thinking, possibly, that they might have been taken to
England, I applied to my friend Rev. Joseph Hunter, of London, a learned antiquary,
and intimately acquainted with the public archives; but he had never seen or heard
of the missing volumes.

† The reason may have been, that the petitioner for naturalization must have
received the sacrament in a Protestant reformed congregation within three months
previous. This would have required him either to become a member of the Episcopal
Church, or else to join a Congregational, Presbyterian, or other dissenting church, —
all of which were hedged in with creeds.

Superior Court of Judicature, from 1741 *to* 1780.—*Naturalizations.*

Upon reading the petition of Nicholas Budd, a native of Norway, in the kingdom of Denmark, but now resident in Boston, showing that by evidences, and a certificate herewith presented, he, conceiving himself to be duly qualified for and entitled to naturalization, according to an Act made in the thirteenth year of his present majesty's reign, and thereupon praying that he may be naturalized according to said Act of Parliament,—*Ordered,* That the prayer of the petition be granted; it appearing to the court that the said Nicholas Budd has been an inhabitant of his majesty's dominions for more than seven years last past, and has within three months last past received the sacrament in a Protestant reformed congregation in this town of Boston. The oaths appointed to be taken instead of the oaths of allegiance and supremacy were administered to him by order of court, and subscribed by him; and he made and subscribed the declaration according to the direction of the said Act of Parliament.

Aaron Lopez, of Swansey, in the county of Bristol, merchant, a Jew, formerly residing at Newport, in the Colony of Rhode Island, &c.,—to wit, at said Newport from Oct. 13, 1752, to Sept. 10, 1762, and at said Swansey since,—took and subscribed the oaths, &c., in presence of the chief justice and other three justices, between the hours of nine and twelve in the morning.*

Emanuel Peraro, a Portuguese, now of Boston, mariner, where he has resided for more than seven years, and not been absent for more than two months, proof made thereof, and of his having received the sacrament according to the usage of the Church of England, was admitted, and took and subscribed the oaths before the chief justice and other justices, between the hours aforesaid.

* Lopez was a Jew. In 1777, with several other Jewish families, he removed to Leicester, in the Province of Massachusetts Bay, and was there extensively engaged in trade. He was a man of intelligence and industry, and became thrifty according to the wont of his people.

See Washburn's History of Leicester for some further account of Lopez and other Jewish residents in that town.

Theodore Dehon, now of Boston, born out of the legiance of his majesty the King of Great Britain, resided in said Boston more than seven years, and not been absent, &c.; that he is a Protestant, and of the communion of the Church of England. And said Theodore, on certificate of his having received the sacrament of the Lord's Supper according to the usage of the church aforesaid, was admitted, and took and subscribed the oaths before the chief justice and two other justices, between the hours, &c.

Turning from the English statutes, it is next to be ascertained whether the Colonial charters clothed the local government with authority to create British subjects within their respective Colonies.

By the Massachusetts-Colony Charter, the governor, assistants, and freemen had power to choose others to be free of the company, and to transport "so many of our loving subjects, or any other strangers that will become our loving subjects and live under our allegiance, as shall willingly accompany them in the same voyages and 'plantation.'" Under this provision of the charter, there would seem to be no difficulty in supposing that they did or might admit foreign Protestants to become freemen. If any such strayed this way, men of orthodox lives and conversation, according to the standard, and were admitted to the church, as they might be, what prevented their being made free, on petition to that end? By joining the church, the door was open which gave a view of civil and political privileges in the near distance. No one could be admitted to freedom, unless he was a member of one of the churches; and, being a member, admission was almost of course, if applied for.* The colonists were still a "company," an incorporated company, with power to

---

* None could be compelled to become freemen; and, after a while, it came to be a sore evil that many church members refrained from applying for admission. They did so that they might not be called to public service as constables, jurors, selectmen, &c. In order to meet their case, a fine was imposed on all such who refused service.— *Colonial Laws*, 1647.

admit or refuse admission as they pleased; in other words, to select associates according to their pleasure and their sympathies, within the prescribed limits. These would then, in the language of the charter, "become our loving subjects, and live under our allegiance." Of course, they would only be subjects within the Colony, with no power to exercise civil and political functions in England. It may be that the case never occurred; but, if it did occur, it is not seen how any other result could have been reached.

In the Province Charter, there was no express provision authorizing the naturalization of foreigners; and none can be gathered by implication.

In New Hampshire, there is nothing on the subject, either in the commission of Charles II. to President Cutts, or in the commission of 6 George III. to Governor Wentworth.

In Rhode Island, the charter of 15 Charles II. authorized the Assembly to choose persons to be free of the company and body politic, and to admit them into the same. The charter made no distinction between English subjects and others.

So, in Connecticut, the charter of Charles II. allowed the General Assembly to choose, &c., persons to be free of the body politic, and to admit them into the same.

In New York, by the letters-patent of 16 Charles II. to the Duke of York, the duke was allowed to bring into the Colony not only subjects of the realm, "but any other strangers who would become subjects." And, when the Province was surrendered to the crown, it was stipulated that "all people should continue free denizens" within the Colony; and "that any people might come from the Netherlands, and plant" in the Province.

In New Jersey, in 1664, under the government of Lord Berkeley and Sir George Carteret, all who wished were admitted to become freemen, and so subjects, on taking the oaths of allegiance, &c. Being *absolute* lords-proprietors, they were not limited in their authority, as were the charter governments.

In Pennsylvania, by the "laws agreed upon in England" in 1683, "every inhabitant purchasing a hundred acres; every person who has paid his passage, and taken a hundred acres; every person that hath been a servant or bondman, and 'is free by his service,' and has taken fifty acres; 'and every inhabitant, artificer, or other resident in the Province, that pays scot or lot * to the governor,'—shall be deemed a freeman, and capable of electing or being elected representative or councillor." †

In Maryland, Lord Baltimore, by the charter of 8 Charles I., was constituted "the true and absolute lord and proprietary," and of course, as such, had the power to authorize his Assembly to grant process of naturalization; which power, as will be seen in the sequel, was exercised.

In North Carolina, no such power was reserved in the charter of Charles II.

The next inquiry is, Did any of the Colonies, in their local Legislatures, establish laws on the subject, or lay claim of right so to do? Mr. Dane, the learned and generally very accurate commentator on American law, states that "there were no naturalizations in the Colonies, before the Revolution, but such as took place under the Acts of the British Parliament." ‡ The remarks before made on the charters show that he is in error; and this will appear beyond question by

---

* Scot *and* lot is defined to be "parish payments."

† Colonial Records, vols. i., xxix., xxx.

‡ Abridgment of American Law, vol. iv. p. 708. Mr. Dane also states, p. 709, that "the Germans who came from Germany, and settled at Waldoborough about A.D. 1750, were and remained aliens." Perhaps this was so: but then it must have been of their own choice; for, so far as they were Protestants,—and most if not all of them were of that faith,—they might have been naturalized under the statute of 13 George II., chap. 7, passed in 1740.

the following reference to the laws of several of the Colonies.

In 1683, "to quiet the minds of his majesty's subjects of foreign birth," the Legislature of New York passed an Act, allowing all persons professing Christianity, now or hereafter becoming inhabitants, to be naturalized on taking the oath of allegiance. This phrase, "all persons professing Christianity," is found in no other Colonial law, and doubtless was introduced because the Duke of York was a Roman Catholic; and the king was well known to be in full sympathy with his brother, though outwardly conforming to the Church of England. Again: by a law of 1715, 1 George I., foreigners who had become inhabitants after 1683, who had purchased estates and conveyed them away, or who had died seized thereof, were deemed to be naturalized; and all Protestant foreigners, inhabitants in 1715, were to be deemed natural subjects on taking the prescribed oaths within nine months from the passage of the Act.*

In New Jersey, as has been seen, Lord Berkeley and Sir George Carteret, in 1664, among their "Grants and Concessions," allowed all who would become subjects to be admitted to become freemen on taking the oaths of allegiance; and authorized the Assembly to pass an Act "to give to all strangers . . . a naturalization, . . . and all such freedoms and privileges within the Province as to his majesty's subjects of right belong." †

And in Pennsylvania, as has been seen, by the laws agreed upon in England in 1683, the most ample power was given in the premises.

So also in Maryland, under the successors of Sir George Calvert, — Lord Baltimore: "The true and absolute lords

---

* Laws of New York, Livingston and Smith's edition, 1762. 2 vols. folio.

† "Grants and Concessions," pp. 13, 14, 17. Folio.

and proprietaries." The same power was vested in the Assembly.*

In Virginia, there was a law of 1671, under which "any strangers"—as the expression was—might be naturalized; and, by virtue of this law, many were naturalized by special Acts of the Assembly. This continued until 1680, when Lord Culpepper brought over, "under the great seal of England," a naturalization law, which was introduced, "and passed the Assembly unanimously."

In October, 1705, another naturalization law was passed. The latter law at least, if not the previous ones, was confined to foreign Protestants; they taking the usual oaths, and the oath of abjuration of "the pretended Prince of Wales."

In 1738, chap. 12, the General Assembly authorized the Governor to grant letters of naturalization to any aliens who should settle on the Roanoke,—the southern boundary of the Colony; they taking the oaths, &c.

In Massachusetts, as before stated, there was neither express nor implied authority in the General Court to pass laws on the subject, nor by special Acts to admit foreigners to the privileges of British subjects.

The statute of Anne, 1708, repealed in 1711, had no reference to the Colonies; and there was no subsequent English statute, until that of 13 George II. in 1740, by which foreigners residing in Massachusetts could become British subjects. Indeed, it was so from the revocation of the Colony Charter until 1740. Meanwhile, many foreign Protestants had settled in Massachusetts,—Huguenots driven from France on the revocation of the edict of Nantes, with Germans and others who had emigrated to this country for the "enlargement of their outward estates." These persons were subjected to the

---

* The law itself has not been found on the old Statute-book. It may have been overlooked. But that the power was freely exercised, appears from statute 1704, chap. 4, regulating for the future the fees which the Clerk of the Assembly should receive from persons naturalized by Acts of the Assembly.

payment of taxes, and sometimes were called to exercise municipal office; but, in all other respects, they were debarred from the rights and privileges of natural-born subjects. They were not numerous in the Puritan Commonwealth, compared with some of the other Colonies; but numerous enough to be considered on that ground, as well as for their general good character and quiet demeanor.

Possibly Massachusetts thought, that if Maryland, Virginia, and other sister Colonies, permitted resident foreigners to become British subjects within their own borders, she might do the same.

Thus circumstanced, several French Protestants, and one from Germany, presented the following petition to the General Court, at the February Session, 1731, N.S.: —

"To His Excellency Jonathan Belcher, Esq., Governor and Commander-in-chief in and over his Majesty's Province of Massachusetts Bay; to the Honorable the Council and the House of Representatives in General Court assembled.

"The petition of the persons hereto subscribed showeth that the petitioners, for the most part, were forced to leave their native country of France on account of the Protestant religion, in which they had been bred up and professed, and for which some of the petitioners have been greatly persecuted and distressed.

"And, farther, the petitioners most humbly remonstrate to your Excellency and to this Great and General Assembly, that the most part of them have, for almost the space of forty years or upwards (during which time they have chiefly resided in this country), behaved themselves justly to their neighbours, and, in their respective callings, with unshaken fidelity towards the gouvernment here, and the crown of Great Britain; and have been allways subjected as well as to pay rates and taxes, as also to bear offices of constable, &c., which several of them have sustained and executed with great faithfulness in their respective dutys: so that they hope, by the favour of this Great and General Court (which is well known at all times to act with great equity, and to relieve, where they can, the distressed), that as they have been always subject to do dutys, so they may be intituled to all the privileges of a denisen, or natural-born subject, of his majesty's, so far as is consistent with the power and justice of this Great and General Court; it being what hath been generally practiced by most nations of Europe in favour of the French‑Protestant refugees, but more particularly by the crown of Great Britain and the dependent Colonys, as the petitioners can prove by many instances. Therefore, upon the whole, the petitioners do humbly pray an order of this Great and General Court to confer upon them the rights and privileges of denisens, or free-born subjects, of the King of Great Britain; or be otherwise relieved, notwithstanding any law, usage, or custom, to the contrary; or that they may be farther heard by the Council in the premises. They say relieved as this Great and General Court shall judge meet; and, as in duty bound, your petitioners shall ever pray, &c.

Andrew Le Mercier.

Daniel Johonnot

Andrew Sigourney Jr. Per

John Peter

Adam Duchezeau

Martin Brimmer

The same favour is humbly Desired By a protestant German Came from Hanover

"In Council, Feb. 25, 1730. — Read, and ordered that the prayer of the petition be so far granted as that the petitioners, together with all other foreign Protestant inhabitants of this Province, shall, within this Province, hold and enjoy all the privileges and immunities of his majesty's natural-born subjects; and that they have leave to bring in a bill accordingly.

"Sent down for concurrence,

"J. WILLARD, *Secretary.*

"In the House of Representatives, Feb. 26, 1730. — Read and concurred.

"J. QUINCY, *Speaker.*"

In pursuance of this leave, a bill was introduced into the House of Representatives, which passed to be enacted on the 16th of March, and was approved by Governor Belcher on the 2d of April following. It is in the following terms; viz. : —

"Passed by the Great and General Court, or Assembly, of his majesty's Province of the Massachusetts Bay, in New England, begun and held at Boston upon Wednesday, the tenth day of February, 1730.

"*Chapter XIV. — An Act for Naturalizing Protestants of Foreign Nations inhabiting within this Province.*

"Whereas divers Protestants of the French and other foreign nations have removed themselves and their families into this Province, who are well affected to his majesty's government, and useful members of the Commonwealth, but, being born out of the king's legiance, have not, by law, a right to the privileges and immunities of his majesty's natural-born subjects, but are under divers disabilities, and subjected to many inconveniences and difficulties in their persons and estates : —

"To the intent, therefore, that such persons, and all other well-disposed Protestants of foreign nations, may have due encouragement to settle themselves and their families within this Province, —

"Be it enacted by his Excellency the Governor, Council, and Representatives in General Court assembled, and by the authority of the same, —

3

"That, from and after the publication of this Act, all Protestants, of foreign nations, that have inhabited or resided within this Province for the space of one year, are hereby declared to be naturalized to all intents, constructions, and purposes whatsoever, within this Province; and from henceforth, and at all times hereafter, shall be entitled to have and enjoy all the rights, liberties, and privileges within this Province, and no otherwise, which his majesty's natural-born subjects in the said Province ought to have and enjoy, as fully to all intents and purposes whatsoever as if they had been born within the said Province.

"Provided always, and it is hereby enacted, That all foreign Protestants that shall have the benefit of this Act shall take the oaths by law appointed to be taken, instead of the oaths of allegiance and supremacy; subscribe the test, or declaration; and take, repeat, and subscribe the abjuration-oath, — in presence of the Governor and Council of this Province; which shall be made of record in the Council-books, and for which each person so swearing and subscribing shall pay to the Secretary of the Province five shillings; and he shall demand no more.

"And be it further enacted by the authority aforesaid, That if any foreign Protestant, having so sworn and subscribed as aforesaid, shall and do demand a certificate of his being entered upon record in manner aforesaid, the Secretary of this Province, for the time being, is hereby directed and required to grant the same under his hand, for which he may demand two shillings and sixpence, and no more; which certificate shall at all times be a sufficient proof that such person is naturalized by this Act, and as effectual as if the record aforesaid were actually produced by them or any of them."

The foregoing Act was passed to be enacted March 16, and was approved by Governor Belcher, April 2, 1731. The session began Feb. 10, and ended April 24, 1731.

It will be observed that this statute gives to those who are naturalized the same rights as natural-born subjects within the Province. Of course, no wider power could be exercised. No Colonial government, as before remarked, could confer rights and privileges to be exercised outside of the local jurisdiction, much less in the mother country. Parliament alone could give authority to widen a Colonial naturalization, so that the subject of it should be a denizen of the empire.*

Under this law, all the petitioners, except Duchezeau, — viz., Le Mercier,† Johonnot,‡ Sigourney,§ Petel,‖ and Brimmer,¶ — appeared before the Governor and Council on the 12th of the same April, and were naturalized. They were followed, on the 7th of December then next, by Philip Bongarden,** John Brown (*nomen generalissimum*), John Saciller, John Groward, and Philip Palier. John Arnault, of Boston, furrier, closed the list on the 18th of August, 1732.

These are all the persons whose names appear on the

---

* In the statute of 7 and 8 Victoria, chap. 6, which freely opened the door for the admission of foreigners, a question is raised, whether the Colonial laws on the subject of naturalization were of any validity. In consequence of this doubt, the statute of 10 and 11 Victoria, chap. 83, was enacted in 1847; confirming all such laws already made, and allowing future laws touching local naturalization, subject to confirmation or disallowance by her majesty. No law of the kind could have any validity beyond the limits of the Colony in which it was made. It was further declared, that the statute of 7 and 8 Victoria, chap. 66, did not extend to the Colonies.

† In his will, dated at Dorchester, Nov. 7, 1761, with a codicil, February, 1764, proved June 15, 1764, he names children, — Andrew, Margaret, Jane, and Bartholomew, "if living." His son Peter Le Mercier, born Aug. 7, 1723, is not named. No examination has been made to ascertain the time of his death. His daughter Jane (unmarried), living in Dorchester, in 1769 conveyed to William Dennie, of Boston, part of an estate, No. 18, Long Wharf, which she inherited from her father. The deed was not recorded till 1798.

‡ "Daniel Johonnot, of Boston, distiller," in his will, May, 1748, proved July 1, 1748, names sons, — Zachary, Andrew, and Francis; and the children of his daughter, Mary Ann (Johonnot) Boyer, deceased.

§ "Andrew Sigourney, sen., of Boston, distiller, aged and infirm," made his will in May, 1736. It was proved July 5, 1748. His children were Andrew (mariner), Susanna, Mary, Charles, Anthony, Daniel, Hannah. His wife Mary survived him.

‖ "John Petel, of Boston, mariner, made his will, June 30, 1735. It was proved May 9, 1749. He was a married man, but left no children.

¶ "Martin Brimmer, of Boston, staymaker," in his will, April 3, 1755, proved June 24, 1760, mentions wife Susanna, and four sons — viz., Herman, Martin, Andrew, and John Baker — and four daughters.

** "Philip Bongarden, of Boston, shopkeeper," made his will, June 24, 1748. It was proved April 20, 1753. He names his wife; his daughter Elizabeth, wife of Æneas Mackay; and his grandson, Philip Cutler. In 1748, he became the owner of some real estate on the northerly side of State Street.

Council-records. Why so few sought the benefit of this law, is not known. The number of foreign Protestants, at least French Protestants, may have been more numerous for a few years after 1687 than they were in 1731; but there were others — respectable men, who might be named — here in the latter year who do not seem to have become subjects of Massachusetts Bay. Perhaps they were naturalized in Great Britain, or in some other of " the dependent colonys " (*ante*, p. 16).

At the present day, descendants of Sigourney, Johonnot, and Brimmer, bear up the respectable character of their earliest American ancestors; while of Groward and Palier no vestiges have been discovered. In May, 1748, Brown and Arnault, two of the proprietors of the French Church in School Street, in connection with the remaining proprietors, — viz., " Stephen Botineau (the only surviving elder of the church), Andrew Le Mercier (clerk, minister of said church), Zechariah Johonnot, Andrew Johonnot, James Packenet, William Bowdoin, and Andrew Sigourney, — conveyed the church-property to the trustees of the new Congregational Church, of which the Rev. Andrew Croswell was pastor.*

Rev. Mr. Le Mercier was successor to Rev. Peter Daillé, who died in May, 1715. The former, surviving the diminution and dissolution of his society, went to his rest, in Boston, in March, 1764. He was held in esteem, in the place of his adoption, for his Christian virtues and graces.†

It only remains to speak of Bongarden and Saciller, and that in connection with the Palatines. Beyond this connection, nothing has been ascertained in relation to Saciller. In March, 1732, Philip Bongarden and John Saciller, as

---

* Drake's History of Boston; Suffolk Registry of Deeds.

† The late Rev. Dr. Holmes published a very interesting "Memoir of the French Protestants, who settled at Oxford, Mass., A.D. 1686; with a Sketch of the entire History of the Protestants of France." See Collections of the Massachusetts Historical Society, vol. ii. 3d series, pp. 1–88.

"agents for the Palatines," made complaint to the Governor and Council of "the cruel and inhuman treatment" the Palatines received "from Captain Jacob Lobb, in their passage from Holland, by reason of which the greatest part of their company died at sea; and of his barbarous usage of the survivors after their arrival at Martha's Vineyard, which had occasioned the death of divers others; and prayed that exemplary justice might be done on the said Lobb." The Council referred the complainants, with their papers, to the Superior Court.

Two indictments were found against Lobb at the April Term of the Superior Court in Barnstable. Lobb was a Cornwall man from Penzance, and was on a voyage from Rotterdam to Philadelphia; having in his vessel more than a hundred Palatines, who went on board at Rotterdam in June, 1731. The vessel was obliged to put into the Vineyard in November, while on the voyage to Philadelphia. Lobb was charged with occasioning the death of Johannes Youngman, about two years of age, son of John Didrick Youngman; and Jacob Comes, jun., about the age of nine years, a Palatine, son of Jacob Comes,—by detaining them on board the vessel after she reached Holmes's Hole; that the child Youngman was infirm and sickly, and languished and died by reason of not being furnished by Lobb with sufficient food to sustain life; and that Comes also died of hunger. According to the allegations in the indictment, Lobb was under contract to supply the passengers with provisions for the voyage. The jury returned verdicts in favor of the captain.

In the latter part of the same month, Bongarden and Saciller made complaint to the Governor and Council of other troubles suffered by the Palatines at Edgartown, inasmuch as Lobb refused to save the town harmless for their support, and the authorities threatened to imprison and sell them to satisfy charges. The Council acted promptly on this complaint.

In July following, Bongarden alone preferred a third petition, by which it appeared that the poor Palatines — now more than a year from home, and still distant from their destination — were in Duke's-County Jail at the suit of Lobb, pending in the Court of Common Pleas; and that Payne and Zaccheus Mayhew, two of the justices, had so far engaged in " the controversy as to be liable to a bias " in Lobb's favor. The Council, on investigation, being satisfied that the Mayhews had taken sides with Lobb, set them aside in all causes between him and the Palatines, and appointed Joseph Lathrop and John Thacher special justices in their place.

In May, 1736, the Council recognized the humanity and fidelity of Philip Bongarden, and allowed him for his " charge, time, and trouble," on account of the Palatines, the sum of £173. 16s.

The law of the Province of Massachusetts, which has been under notice, is not found in any edition of the general laws; so that its existence seems to be unknown at the present day. The Province Charter required that all laws should be transmitted to the king, " under the public seal, . . . for approbation or disallowance." If disallowed and rejected by the king in Privy Council, within three years after being presented, and so signified under the king's " sign-manual and signet," or " by the Privy Council to the Governor," they became thenceforth " void, and of none effect; " but, if not returned within three years, they remained in force.

There is nothing to be found in the office of the Secretary of State to show that this law was returned to the Governor, except the fact that the law appears nowhere, save in a little pamphlet of temporary enactments. This, however, may be considered full proof; and, as there was no naturalization after that of Arnault in August, 1732, it is a fair inference that the law soon afterwards came to an untimely death.

It is a matter of history that Provincial laws were disallowed by the king; and how then can it be accounted for that no veto or disallowance thereof, "under the king's sign-manual or signet," or "by the Privy Council to the Governor," is to be found on file, or in any way alluded to, in the records at the office of the Secretary of the Commonwealth? *

It only remains to consider the subject of naturalization in Massachusetts, from the date of the Declaration of Independence until near the close of the last century, — six years after the adoption of the Constitution of the United States.

By the Declaration of Independence, the Colonies assumed the position of independent States; and, under the Confederation, several of them passed naturalization laws, while others naturalized foreigners by special Acts. There was no uniform system.

"The dissimilarity in the rules of naturalization," says Mr. Madison, "has long been remarked as a fault in our system, and as laying a foundation for intricate and delicate questions." In referring to the confusion of language in the fourth article of the Confederation, he adds, "In one State, residence for a short time confers all the rights of citizenship; in another, qualifications of greater importance are required. An alien, therefore, legally incapacitated for certain rights in the latter, may, by previous residence only in the former, elude his incapacity, and thus the laws of one State be preposterously rendered paramount to the law of another within the jurisdiction of the other." †

This dissimilarity in the rules " gave rise, under the Confederation, to some intricate and delicate questions." ‡

---

* I have found no reason assigned for the disallowance of this law. Was it from any known or supposed difference between the charter governments and the proprietary and royal governments in this respect? We have seen that other Colonies exercised the jurisdiction; and the Huguenots themselves say in their petition (*ante*, p. 16), that many of their brethren have been naturalized by "the dependent Colonys" of Great Britain, "as the petitioners can prove by many instances."

† The Federalist, No. xlii.

‡ Duer's Lectures on Constitutional Jurisprudence, p. 296.

There was no general naturalization law in Massachusetts under the Constitution of 1780; but individuals were admitted to citizenship by special Acts, the earliest of which was June 27, 1782. It appeared in this case that Michael Cunningham and John Prescott, late of Halifax, in Nova Scotia, "had exerted themselves for the relief of American prisoners at Halifax, and, in many instances, opposed British tyranny; espousing the cause of America, and fleeing to this country to pay obedience to, and receive protection from, its laws." As a reward, and "to encourage such well-disposed foreigners to join themselves to us," — "on taking and subscribing the oaths of allegiance, abjuration, and other oaths required by the laws of the Commonwealth, before any two Justices of the Peace," — Cunningham and Prescott "were to be deemed, adjudged, and taken to be, natural subjects of the Commonwealth, to all intents, &c., as if they had been born in the Commonwealth."

The Justices were required to make return to the Secretary of the Commonwealth, "who shall record the same in a book, to be kept among the public records of the Commonwealth for the purpose of recording the names of such foreigners as shall be hereafter naturalized by Acts of the Commonwealth."

The following persons were allowed to be naturalized; but whether they all took the oaths, and actually became subjects or citizens, it is not easy to ascertain, as the book kept by the secretary cannot now be found.* No particular length of residence was required before naturalization. Several of these individuals and families, residents in Boston, will be recognized by those familiar with the society of the place in the earlier part of the present century.†

---

* The title of this book is found in the catalogue kept at the office of the Secretary of State; but the book itself has not been seen for some years.

† Many notes might be made in addition to those which follow, were it worth while to pursue the investigation.

Among those naturalized, there were several persons who had left the State during the Revolution, and adhered to the crown, or, in the words of the statute, had "joined the enemies of the State." In the heat of the war, — September, 1778, — an Act was passed forbidding their return to the State, and providing for their removal in case of return. Should they voluntarily come into the State a second time, "without leave from the General Court," they were, "on conviction before the Superior Court, to suffer the pains of death, without benefit of clergy."

All those persons who left the Province after the 5th of October, 1774, and before the "making" of the Constitution of the Commonwealth, and had taken English protection, were held to be aliens. By a law of 1784, these persons, if not named in the Confiscation Act of 1779, and not having borne arms against their country, might return to the State, under license from the Governor and Council. This license remained in force until the end of the next session of the General Court; at which time, unless the General Court had approved the license, or an Act of naturalization had been passed in favor of the individual, he was required "to depart the State."

1782, June 27. Michael Cunningham, John Prescott.
1784, Feb. 13. John Gardiner, barrister-at-law. John Silvester John* and William Gardiner, his children. [His wife, Ann Gardiner, is mentioned in the title of the Act, but was omitted in the enacting clause. The omission was supplied Oct. 25, 1787.]
Mar. 23. Thomas Hopkins, of Falmouth, Cumberland County, late of Devonshire, Great Britain.
June 30. Thomas Robison, of Falmouth, Cumberland County, late of Quebec.
1785, Feb. 28. Nicholas Rousselet, Boston, auctioneer.
George Smith, Andover, laborer.

---

* The late Rev. Dr. Gardiner, of Trinity Church, Boston.

1785, Nov. 22. Paul Beltremieux, Newburyport, late of Rochelle, France.

   „ 23. William Bond, Falmouth, Cumberland County, goldsmith, late of Devonshire, in Great Britain.

1786, Feb. 7. Michael Walsh, Salisbury.

   „ 8. William Erving, Esq., Boston.

        John Duballet,* Boston.

   „ 17. James Wakefield, born in Massachusetts, but for fifteen years past residing in Nova Scotia. Ann Wakefield, his wife. Their children, — Benjamin, Ann, Terence,† Mary.

June 5. Robert Morris, Shrewsbury.

       James Alexander, Shrewsbury.

July 7. Jonathan Curson, Northampton, late of Exeter, England.

       William Oliver, Northampton, late of Bridport, England.

1787, Mar. 2. William Martin and Elizabeth Martin, Boston.

       William Moch,‡ Boston.

       John Amory,§ Boston.

       David Smith, and Elizabeth his wife, Portland. Their children, — Moses, Ruth, Mercy, Lendall, David, Elizabeth, Hannah, Dorothy, Godfrey.

       William Molton, Portland.

       William Haggett, „

       John Nicholas Rudberg, and Anne his wife, Portland.

       Thomas Craigie, Billerica.

May 1. Edward Wyer,‖ and Alice his wife. "His" children, — Edward and William.

       David Greene, and Rebecca his wife. "His" children, — John Rose Greene, David Ireland Greene,¶ Charles Winston Greene,** Rebecca Greene.

---

* Merchant, Distil-house Square. — *Boston Directory*, 1789.

† For many years a druggist and apothecary in Boston.

‡ Hairdresser, 28, Newbury Street. — *Boston Directory*, 1789. By statute 1807, chap. 122, his son William was allowed to take the name of Andrew Jeremiah Allen.

§ Storekeeper, 41, Marlborough Street. — *Boston Directory*, 1789.

‖ He was a physician in Boston, held in great esteem. There are many living who remember his son Edward.

¶ Harvard College, 1800.   ** Harvard College, 1802.

1787, May 1. Thomas English.*

Oct. 29. Bartholomy de Gregoire,† and Maria Theresa his wife. Their children, — Pierre de Gregoire, Nicholas de Gregoire, Maria de Gregoire.

Nov. 16. Alexander Moore, Boston, merchant.

Isaac Smith, „ clerk.

John Deverell, „ silversmith.

John Gregory, „ merchant.

David Poignand, „ merchant, and Delicia his wife.

Abraham Bazin, „ merchant.

Henry Smith, „ merchant, and Elizabeth, his wife. Henry Lloyd Smith, Elizabeth, Catherina, Rebecca, and Anna Smith.

Benjamin Pickman, Esq., Salem.

William Pratt,‡ Boston, merchant, from London.

Kirk Boot,‡ „ „ „ „
Mary, his wife; Frances, their daughter.

1788, June 19. William Menzies Douglass, late of Great Britain.

Paul Crocker, and Lydia his wife. Their grand-children, — Joanna Crocker Chute, Paul Crocker Chute, George Washington Chute, Lunenburg, late of Annapolis, in Nova Scotia.

---

* A merchant, No. 11, Long Wharf. — *Boston Directory*, 1789. He was the father of James L. English, Esq., of Boston.

† Madame Gregoire came to America with a letter of introduction from Lafayette to General Knox, dated Paris, Aug. 1, 1786. "I thought," says the marquis, "my best way was to introduce her to you, who can, better than any one else, advise her how to act, and give her accounts of the frontier, where she says she has some property."

This lady was a grand-daughter of Mons. La Motte Cadillac, to whom the King of France granted a patent of the Island of Mount Desert in 1691. Under this patent, Madam Gregoire claimed the island. "It would seem," says Williamson (History of Maine, vol. ii. p. 515), "to have been a claim too antiquated and obsolete to be regarded: but the government was so highly disposed at this time 'to cultivate mutual confidence and union between the subjects of his most Christian majesty and the citizens of this State,' that the General Court were induced first to naturalize the petitioners and their family, and then quit-claim to them all the interest the Commonwealth had to the island; reserving only, to actual settlers, lots of one hundred acres."

The whole island had been confiscated, in the Revolution, as the property of Governor Bernard; but, as his son John had been a consistent Whig throughout the war, the Commonwealth restored to him *one-half* of it. — *Ibid.*

‡ Messrs. Pratt and Boot, from moderate beginnings, became extensively engaged in mercantile business.

1788, June 19. François Bertodi, of the kingdom of Prussia.*

Nov. 21. Elisha Bourn, Sandwich, late subject of Great Britain.

Seth Perry, „ „ „ „ „ „

Edward Bourn, „ „ „ „ „ „

Richard Devereux, Parsonfield, late of Ireland.

William Jolly, Portland, late of St. Pierre, Martinico.

Jeremiah Joakim Khaler, Boston, late subject of Denmark.

Phillip Theobald, Pownalborough, from Hesse Hannau.

John de Polerisky, „ late of Molsheim, in Alsatia, France.

1789, Feb. 14. James Huyman,† Boston, late of Rotterdam.

James Henry Laugier de Tassy, Boston, late of the Seven United Provinces.

Samuel Weston, Boston, late of the Island of Madeira.

John Hicks, and Fanny Hicks his daughter, Boston.

Frederick William Geyer, Boston.

Charles Vaughan, Hallowell.

William Davis, Windsor, Berkshire, late of Great Britain.

James Scobie, Marblehead, late of Scotland.

Daniel Wright, and Katy his wife, Salem, late of Great Britain.

Nathaniel Chandler, Petersham.

June 22. Nathaniel Skinner,‡ Boston, late of London.

James Scott,§ Boston, native of Great Britain.

James Scott, jun., „ „ „ „ „

George Shinnits, „ „ „ Prussia.

Martin Coning, „ late of Amsterdam.

Akurs Sisson, Dartmouth.

1790, Mar. 1. John Jarvis.

Lewis Leprilete.‖

John Fowler.

---

* In the Act of naturalization, Dr. Bertodi is called of "Persia;" a typographical error for "Prussia." He left a son, who, I believe, is the sole representative of the name in this country.

† Merchant, Foster's Wharf. — *Boston Directory*, 1789.

‡ He was a merchant.   § The second husband of Madam Hancock.

‖ Dr. Leprilete resided at Jamaica Plain.

1790, Mar. 1. Alexander McDonald.

William Welch.*

Peter Le Mercier, and his children, — Polly Eugenia, Sophia Cecile, and Peter Oliver Le Mercier.†

Thomas Lane.

William Cleland.‡

John Pennell.

John Bond.

Mar. 6. John Montgomery.

James Green.

Nathan Kelley.

Stephen Jones.

Thomas Ramsden.

John Sockman.

1791, Mar. 11. John White.

Roger Dickinson.

John Atkinson, and Elizabeth his wife. "His" children, — John Atkinson, jun., Charles Atkinson, Eliza Storer Atkinson, George Hodgson Atkinson, Mary Ann Atkinson, Caroline Frances Atkinson, and William Atkinson.

1793, Mar. 9. George William Erving.§

Sept. 28. Pierre Briamant, Boston.

1794, Feb. 27. Henry Huetson Pentland.

June 24. Thomas Neil.‖

Robert Getty.‖

Robert Holt.

---

* Father of the late John Welch, Esq.

† Thus the names stand in the Act of naturalization. But their names, I suppose, are more correctly given in the record of their guardianship, in Suffolk, in March, 1802; viz., "Eugene Sophia, Cecile Charlotte, and Peter Olivier Lemercier." They were then placed under the guardianship of Earl Sturtevant. Eugene and Cecile were over fourteen years of age, and Peter Olivier under fourteen. The father, perhaps a grandson of the minister, is entitled "Peter Lemercier, late of France, deceased."

In March, 1828, Eugene Sophia, "widow of George C. Flynn;" Cecile Charlotte, "wife of Henry Williams, of Boston;" and Peter Olivier Lemercier, — discharged the bond of guardianship. Williams was well known as a portrait painter.

‡ A broker in Boston.

§ He was educated at Oxford. He was consul at London, and afterwards was appointed ambassador to Spain by Mr. Jefferson.

‖ Traders in Boston.

The Legislature passed a law, June 9, 1792, allowing all persons, proscribed under any of the laws of the State, to be naturalized in the same manner and on the same conditions as provided for other aliens by the Act of Congress "establishing an uniform rule of naturalization," 1790, chap. 3.

It will be observed by the foregoing list that the Legislature of Massachusetts continued to naturalize "aliens" as late as the June Session in the year 1794, — more than four years after Congress had made provision for naturalization, pursuant to the power contained in the Constitution of the United States. This may have been because the Legislature did not consider the power to be exclusive in Congress; * or because there may have been a question, whether the statute of 1790 was prospective, — the provision being, "that any alien, being a free white person, who *shall have resided* within the limits and under the jurisdiction of the United States for the term of two years," &c. The next statute, 1795, chap. 20, was prospective as well as retrospective; and, after its passage, Massachusetts ceased from all further exercise of jurisdiction.

---

* Indeed, so late as 1817, in the Supreme Court of the United States, counsel, in arguing a question in relation to the Maryland law of naturalization, 1780, intimated "that the respective States still preserve the right of making naturalization, giving certain civil rights to foreigners, without conferring political citizenship." Chirac *vs.* Chirac. — *Wheaton's Reports*, vol. ii. p. 264. The court, however, held that the exclusive power of Congress was incontrovertible.